W9-BNR-945

MOON GIRL AND DEVIL DINOSAUR

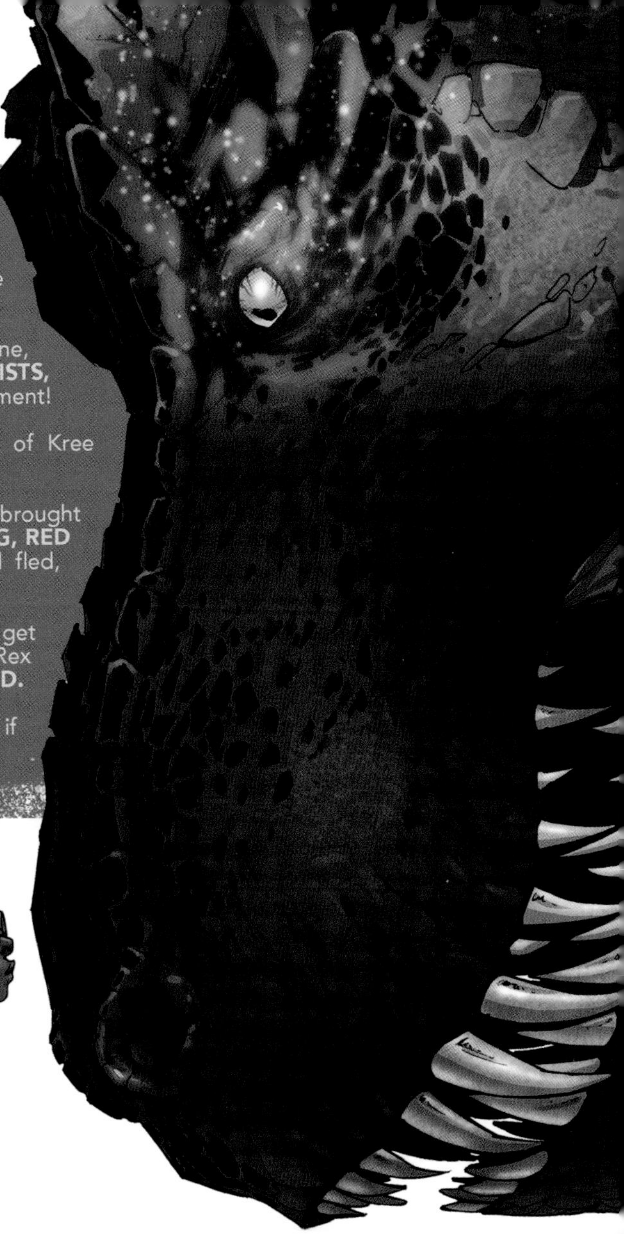

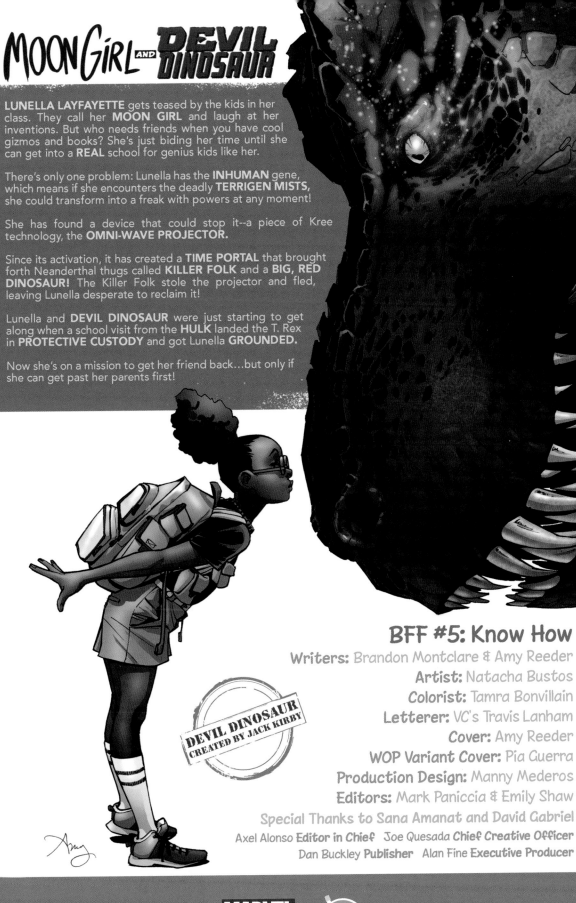

LUNELLA LAYFAYETTE gets teased by the kids in her class. They call her **MOON GIRL** and laugh at her inventions. But who needs friends when you have cool gizmos and books? She's just biding her time until she can get into a **REAL** school for genius kids like her.

There's only one problem: Lunella has the **INHUMAN** gene, which means if she encounters the deadly **TERRIGEN MISTS,** she could transform into a freak with powers at any moment!

She has found a device that could stop it--a piece of Kree technology, the **OMNI-WAVE PROJECTOR.**

Since its activation, it has created a **TIME PORTAL** that brought forth Neanderthal thugs called **KILLER FOLK** and a **BIG, RED DINOSAUR!** The Killer Folk stole the projector and fled, leaving Lunella desperate to reclaim it!

Lunella and **DEVIL DINOSAUR** were just starting to get along when a school visit from the **HULK** landed the T. Rex in **PROTECTIVE CUSTODY** and got Lunella **GROUNDED.**

Now she's on a mission to get her friend back...but only if she can get past her parents first!

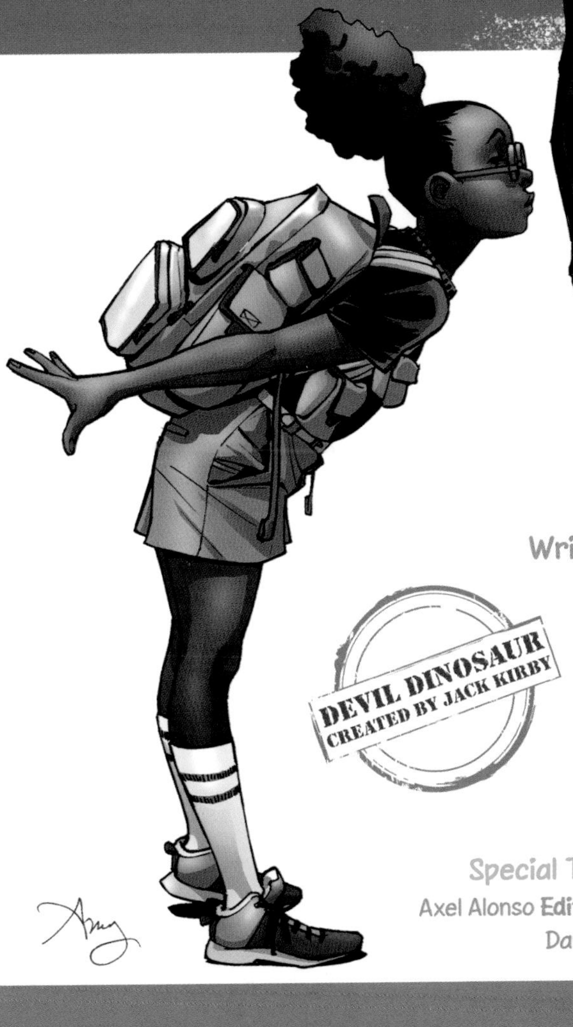

DEVIL DINOSAUR CREATED BY JACK KIRBY

BFF #5: Know How

Writers: Brandon Montclare & Amy Reeder
Artist: Natacha Bustos
Colorist: Tamra Bonvillain
Letterer: VC's Travis Lanham
Cover: Amy Reeder
WOP Variant Cover: Pia Guerra
Production Design: Manny Mederos
Editors: Mark Paniccia & Emily Shaw

Special Thanks to Sana Amanat and David Gabriel

Axel Alonso **Editor in Chief** Joe Quesada **Chief Creative Officer**
Dan Buckley **Publisher** Alan Fine **Executive Producer**

MARVEL
marvelkids.com

ABDO Spotlight

ABDOPUBLISHING.COM

Reinforced library bound edition published in 2018 by Spotlight,
a division of ABDO, PO Box 398166, Minneapolis, Minnesota 55439.
Spotlight produces high-quality reinforced library bound editions for
schools and libraries. Published by agreement with Marvel Characters, Inc.

Printed in the United States of America, North Mankato, Minnesota.
042017
092017

THIS BOOK CONTAINS
RECYCLED MATERIALS

marvelkids.com
© 2017 MARVEL

PUBLISHER'S CATALOGING IN PUBLICATION DATA

Names: Reeder, Amy ; Montclare, Brandon, authors. | Bustos, Natacha ; Bonvillain,
    Tamra, illustrators.
Title: Know how / writers: Amy Reeder ; Brandon Montclare ; art: Natacha Bustos ;
    Tamra Bonvillain.
Description: Reinforced library bound edition. | Minneapolis, Minnesota : Spotlight,
    2018. | Series: Moon Girl and Devil Dinosaur ; BFF #5
Summary: Lunella promises to behave and fit in at school, but her parents are
    unaware of Moon Girl's top secret mission to break Devil Dinosaur out of
    protective custody.
Identifiers: LCCN 2016961928 | ISBN 9781532140129 (lib. bdg.)
Subjects: LCSH: Schools--Juvenile fiction. | Adventure and adventurers--Juvenile
    fiction. | Comic Books, strips, etc.--Juvenile fiction. | Graphic novels--Juvenile
    fiction.
Classification: DDC 741.5--dc23
LC record available at https://lccn.loc.gov/2016961928

Spotlight

A Division of ABDO
abdopublishing.com

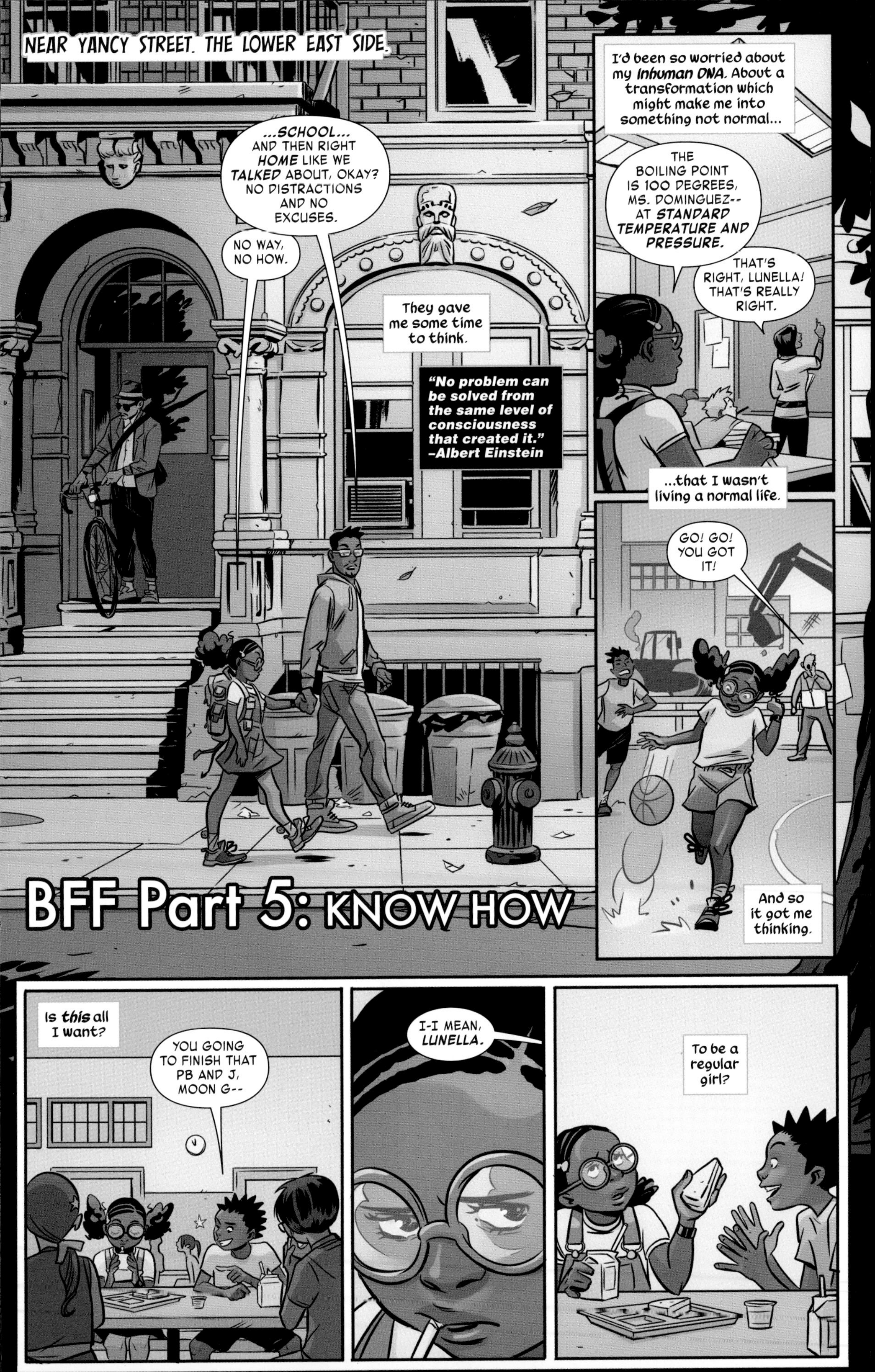

NEAR YANCY STREET. THE LOWER EAST SIDE.
...SCHOOL... AND THEN RIGHT HOME LIKE WE TALKED ABOUT, OKAY? NO DISTRACTIONS AND NO EXCUSES.
NO WAY, NO HOW.
They gave me some time to think.
"No problem can be solved from the same level of consciousness that created it." –Albert Einstein
BFF Part 5: KNOW HOW
I'd been so worried about my Inhuman DNA. About a transformation which might make me into something not normal...
THE BOILING POINT IS 100 DEGREES, MS. DOMINGUEZ-- AT STANDARD TEMPERATURE AND PRESSURE.
THAT'S RIGHT, LUNELLA! THAT'S REALLY RIGHT.
...that I wasn't living a normal life.
GO! GO! YOU GOT IT!
And so it got me thinking.
Is this all I want?
YOU GOING TO FINISH THAT PB AND J, MOON G--
I-I MEAN, LUNELLA.
To be a regular girl?

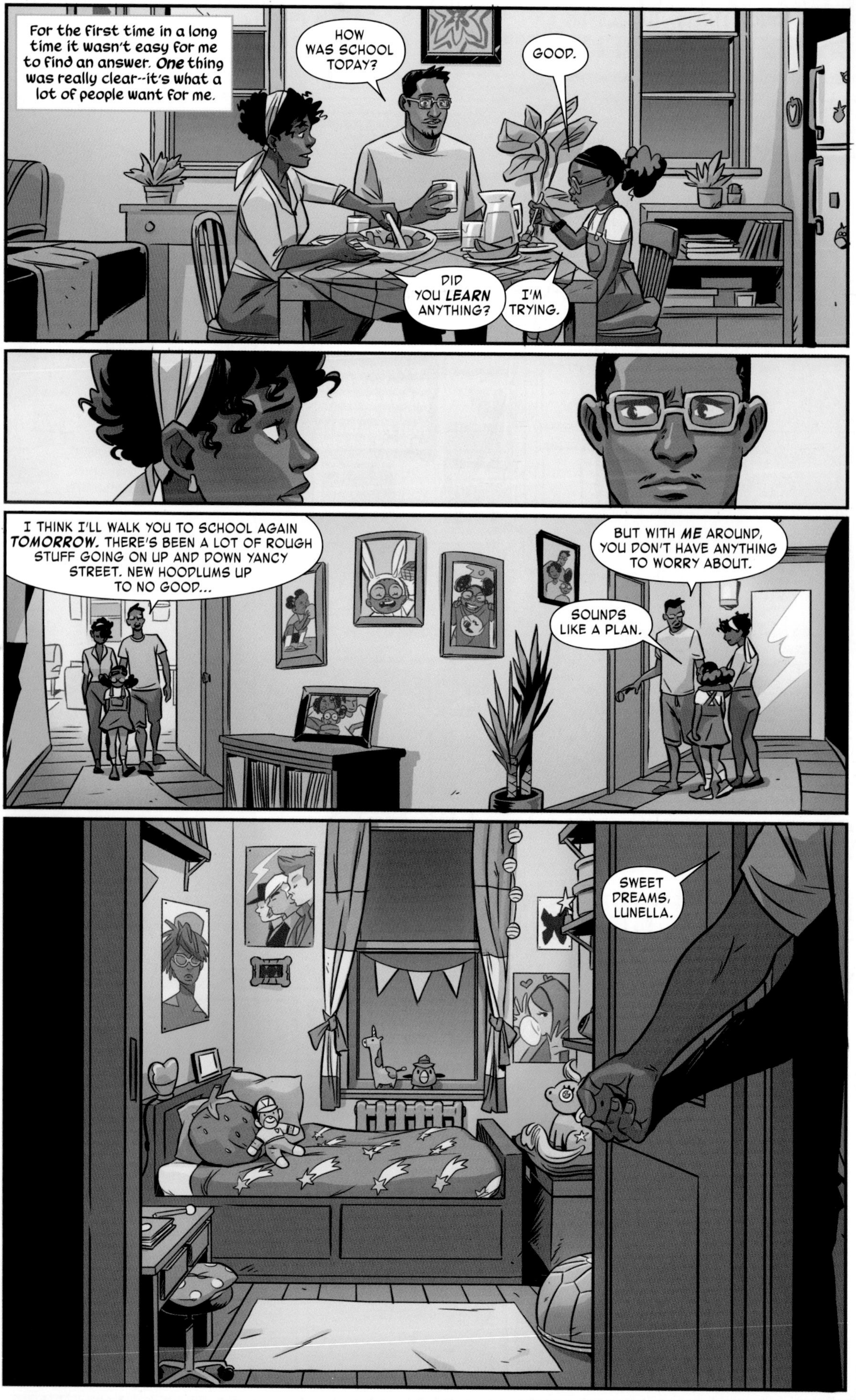

For the first time in a long time it wasn't easy for me to find an answer. *One* thing was really clear--it's what a lot of people want for me.
HOW WAS SCHOOL TODAY?
GOOD.
DID YOU **LEARN** ANYTHING?
I'M TRYING.
I THINK I'LL WALK YOU TO SCHOOL AGAIN **TOMORROW.** THERE'S BEEN A LOT OF ROUGH STUFF GOING ON UP AND DOWN YANCY STREET. NEW HOODLUMS UP TO NO GOOD...
BUT WITH **ME** AROUND, YOU DON'T HAVE ANYTHING TO WORRY ABOUT.
SOUNDS LIKE A PLAN.
SWEET DREAMS, LUNELLA.

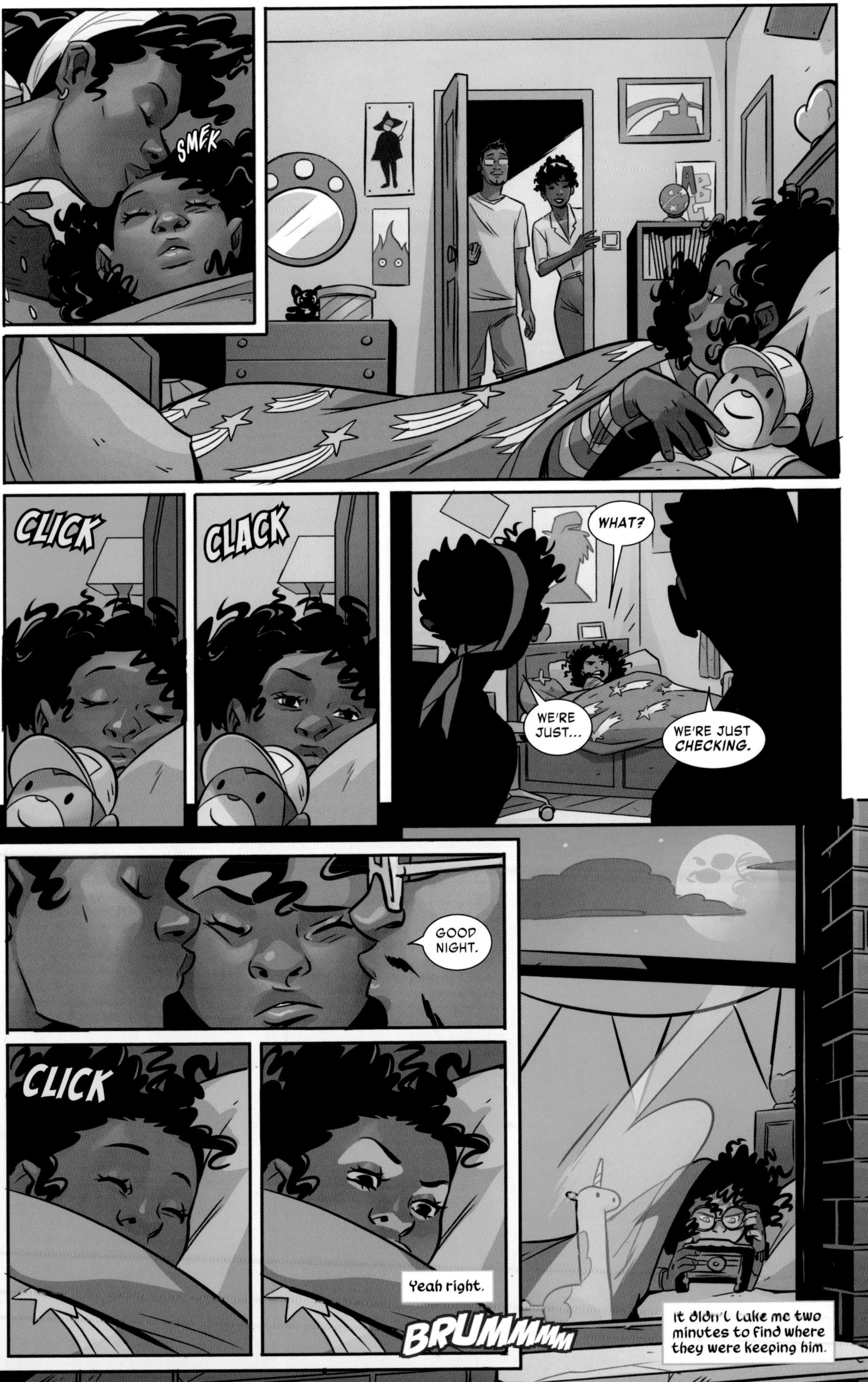
SMEK
CLICK
CLACK
WHAT?
WE'RE JUST...
WE'RE JUST CHECKING.
GOOD NIGHT.
CLICK
Yeah right.
BRUMMMMM
It didn't take me two minutes to find where they were keeping him.

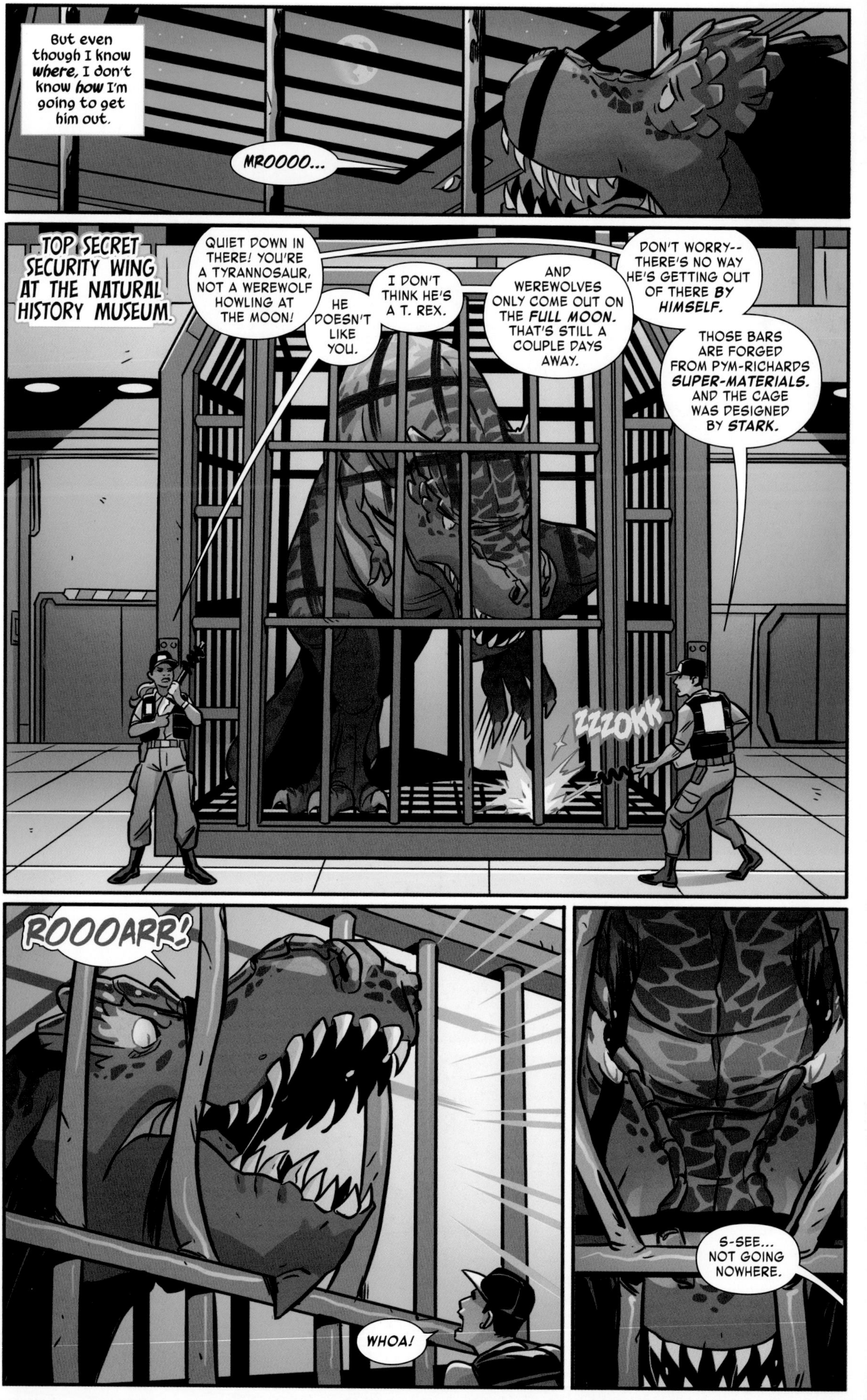
But even though I know *where*, I don't know *how* I'm going to get him out.
MROOOO...
TOP SECRET SECURITY WING AT THE NATURAL HISTORY MUSEUM.
QUIET DOWN IN THERE! YOU'RE A TYRANNOSAUR, NOT A WEREWOLF HOWLING AT THE MOON!
HE DOESN'T LIKE YOU.
I DON'T THINK HE'S A T. REX.
AND WEREWOLVES ONLY COME OUT ON THE *FULL MOON*. THAT'S STILL A COUPLE DAYS AWAY.
DON'T WORRY-- THERE'S NO WAY HE'S GETTING OUT OF THERE *BY HIMSELF*.
THOSE BARS ARE FORGED FROM PYM-RICHARDS *SUPER-MATERIALS*. AND THE CAGE WAS DESIGNED BY *STARK*.
ZZZOKK
ROOOARR!
WHOA!
S-SEE... NOT GOING NOWHERE.

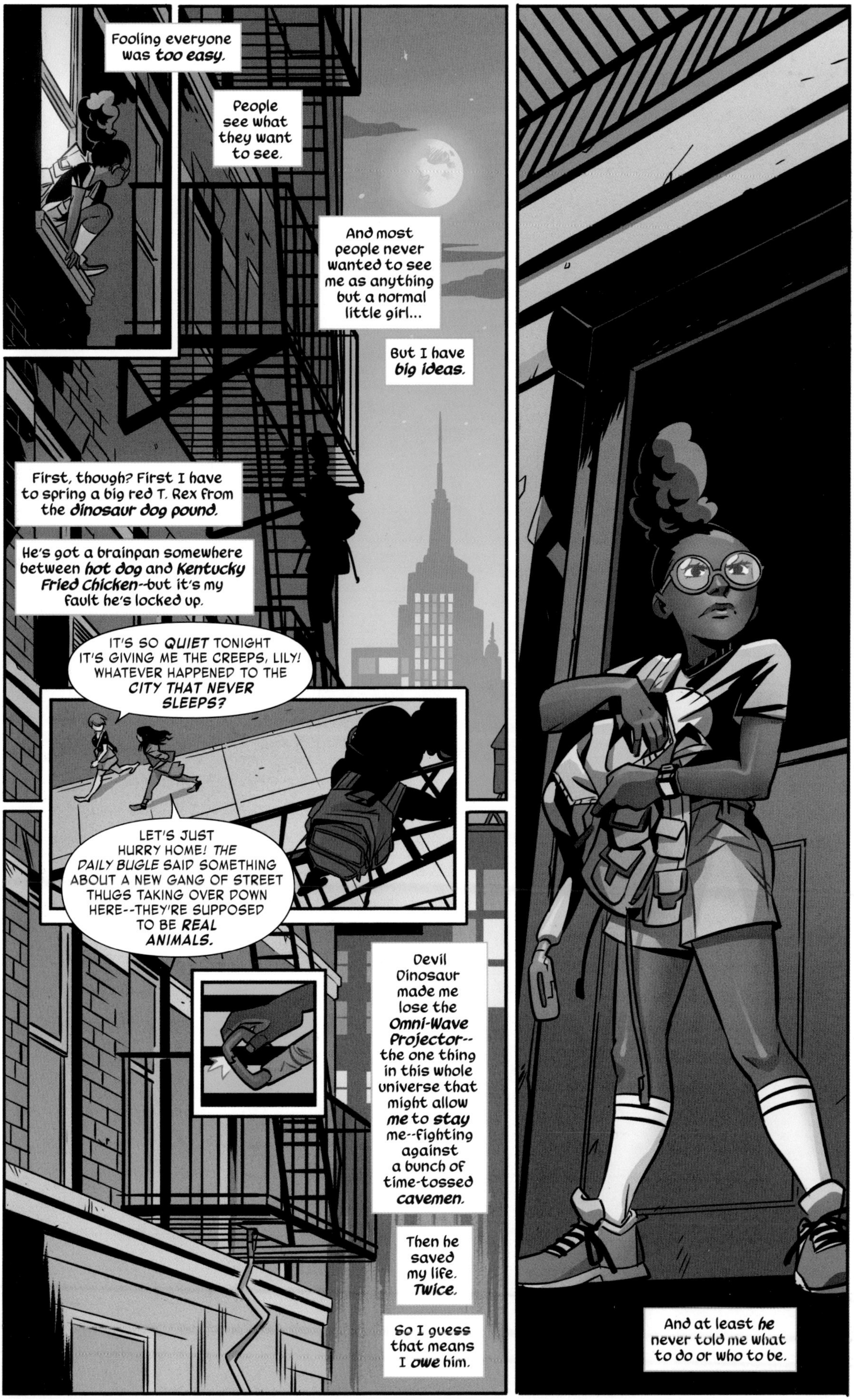

Fooling everyone was too easy.
People see what they want to see.
And most people never wanted to see me as anything but a normal little girl...
But I have big ideas.
First, though? First I have to spring a big red T. Rex from the dinosaur dog pound.
He's got a brainpan somewhere between hot dog and Kentucky Fried Chicken--but it's my fault he's locked up.
IT'S SO QUIET TONIGHT IT'S GIVING ME THE CREEPS, LILY! WHATEVER HAPPENED TO THE CITY THAT NEVER SLEEPS?
LET'S JUST HURRY HOME! THE DAILY BUGLE SAID SOMETHING ABOUT A NEW GANG OF STREET THUGS TAKING OVER DOWN HERE--THEY'RE SUPPOSED TO BE REAL ANIMALS.
Devil Dinosaur made me lose the Omni-Wave Projector--the one thing in this whole universe that might allow me to stay me--fighting against a bunch of time-tossed cavemen.
Then he saved my life. Twice.
So I guess that means I owe him.
And at least he never told me what to do or who to be.

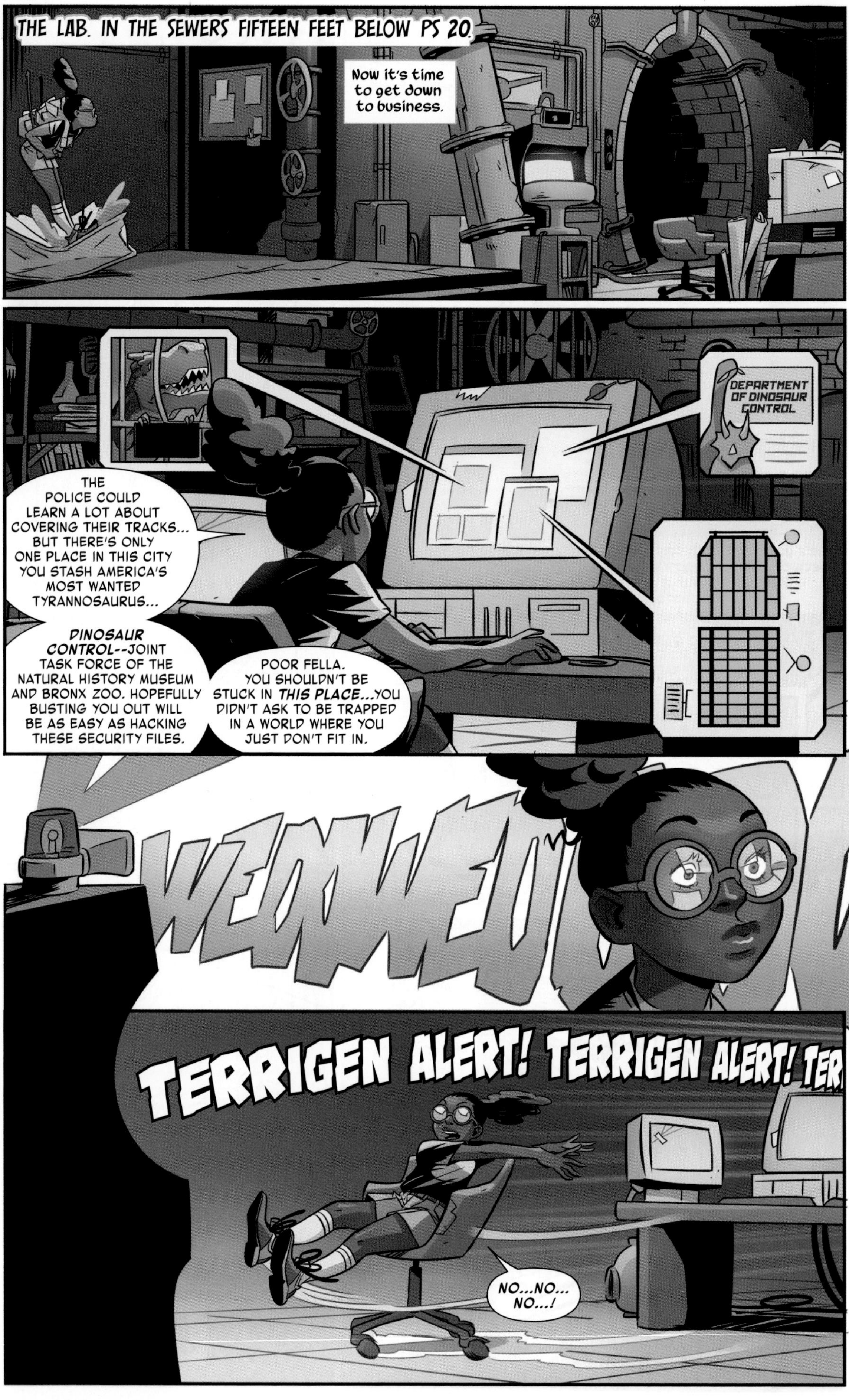
THE LAB. IN THE SEWERS FIFTEEN FEET BELOW PS 20.
Now it's time to get down to business.
DEPARTMENT OF DINOSAUR CONTROL
THE POLICE COULD LEARN A LOT ABOUT COVERING THEIR TRACKS... BUT THERE'S ONLY ONE PLACE IN THIS CITY YOU STASH AMERICA'S MOST WANTED TYRANNOSAURUS...
DINOSAUR CONTROL--JOINT TASK FORCE OF THE NATURAL HISTORY MUSEUM AND BRONX ZOO. HOPEFULLY BUSTING YOU OUT WILL BE AS EASY AS HACKING THESE SECURITY FILES.
POOR FELLA. YOU SHOULDN'T BE STUCK IN *THIS PLACE*...YOU DIDN'T ASK TO BE TRAPPED IN A WORLD WHERE YOU JUST DON'T FIT IN.
TERRIGEN ALERT! TERRIGEN ALERT! TER
NO...NO... NO...!

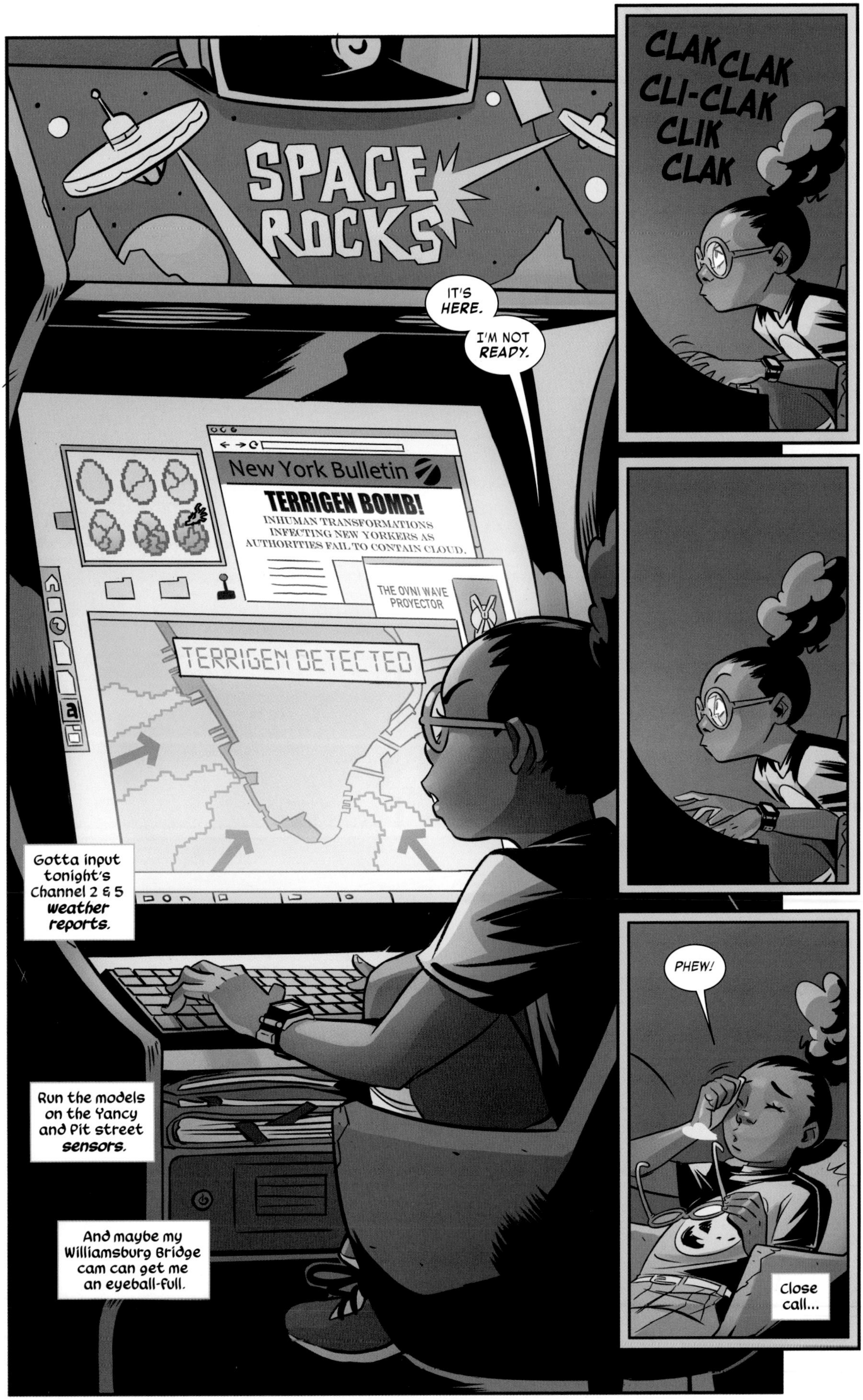
SPACE ROCKS
New York Bulletin
TERRIGEN BOMB!
INHUMAN TRANSFORMATIONS INFECTING NEW YORKERS AS AUTHORITIES FAIL TO CONTAIN CLOUD.
THE OVNI WAVE PROYECTOR
TERRIGEN DETECTED
IT'S HERE.
I'M NOT READY.
Gotta input tonight's Channel 2 & 5 weather reports.
Run the models on the Yancy and Pit street sensors.
And maybe my Williamsburg Bridge cam can get me an eyeball-full.
CLAK CLAK CLI-CLAK CLIK CLAK
PHEW!
Close call...

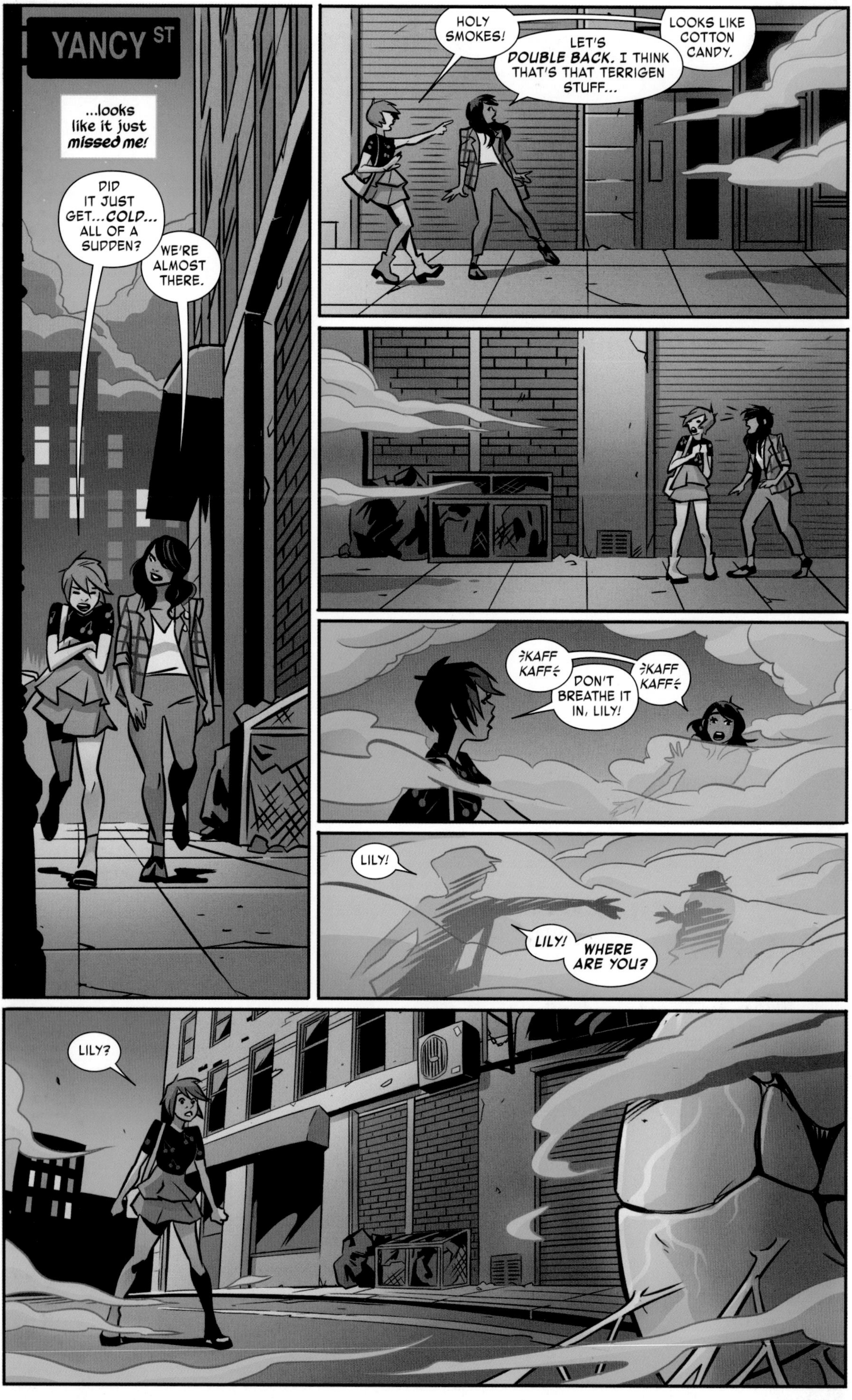
YANCY ST
...looks like it just *missed me!*
DID IT JUST GET...**COLD**... ALL OF A SUDDEN?
WE'RE ALMOST THERE.
HOLY SMOKES!
LOOKS LIKE COTTON CANDY.
LET'S **DOUBLE BACK.** I THINK THAT'S THAT TERRIGEN STUFF...
KAFF KAFF
KAFF KAFF
DON'T BREATHE IT IN, LILY!
LILY!
LILY! **WHERE ARE YOU?**
LILY?

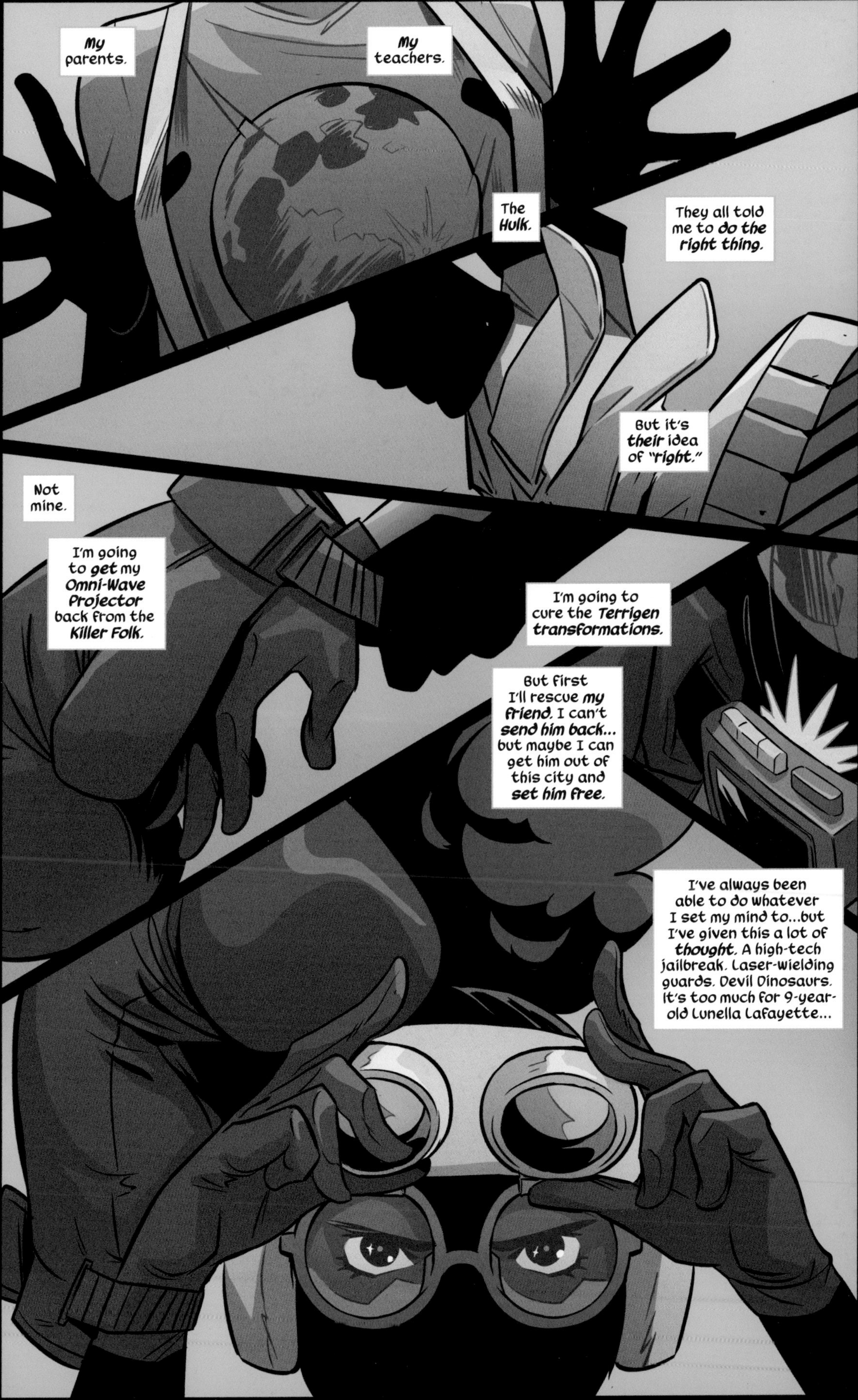
My parents.
My teachers.
The Hulk.
They all told me to do the right thing.
But it's their idea of "right."
Not mine.
I'm going to get my Omni-Wave Projector back from the Killer Folk.
I'm going to cure the Terrigen transformations.
But first I'll rescue my friend. I can't send him back... but maybe I can get him out of this city and set him free.
I've always been able to do whatever I set my mind to...but I've given this a lot of thought. A high-tech jailbreak. Laser-wielding guards. Devil Dinosaurs. It's too much for 9-year-old Lunella Lafayette...

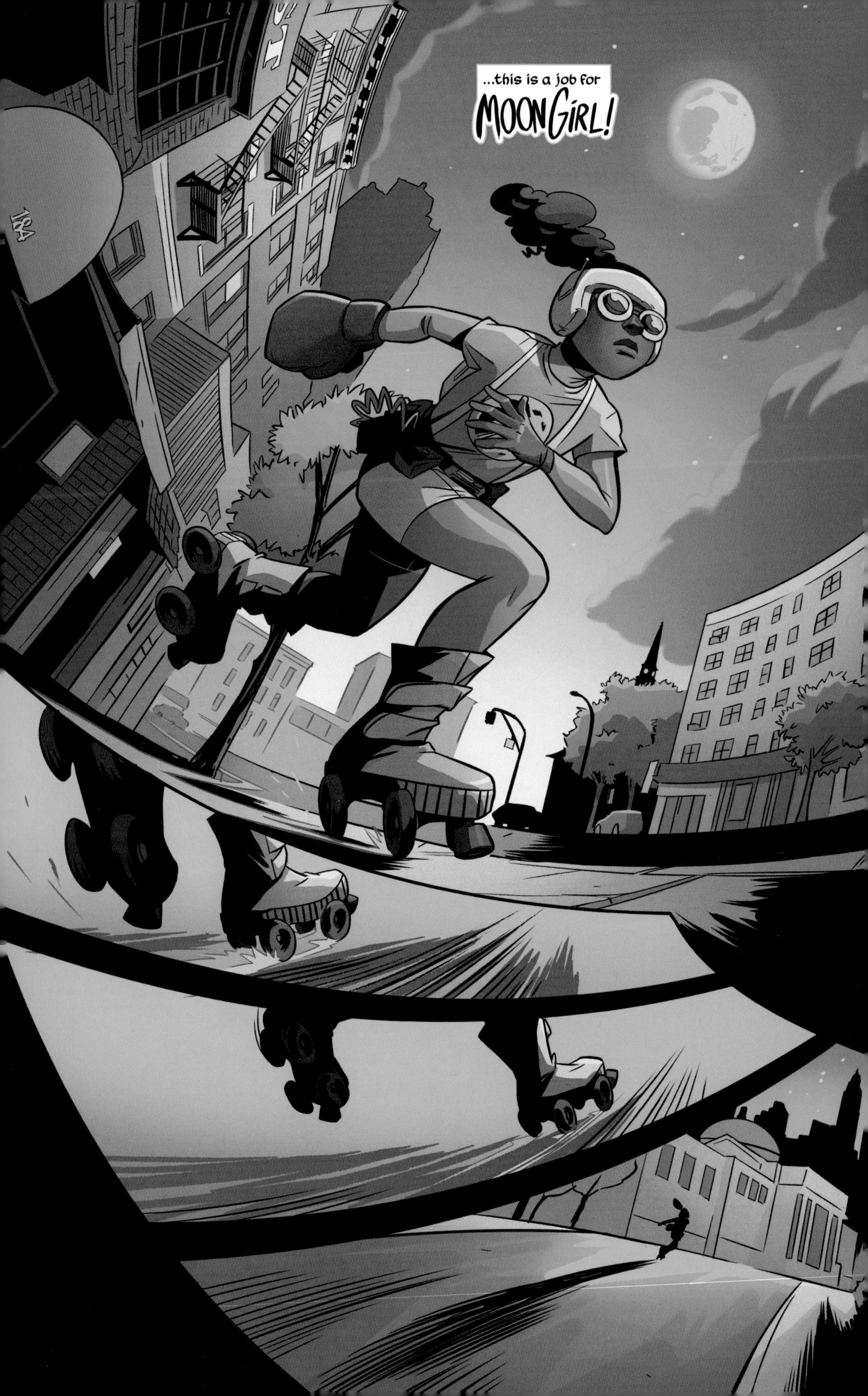
...this is a job for
MOON GIRL!
184

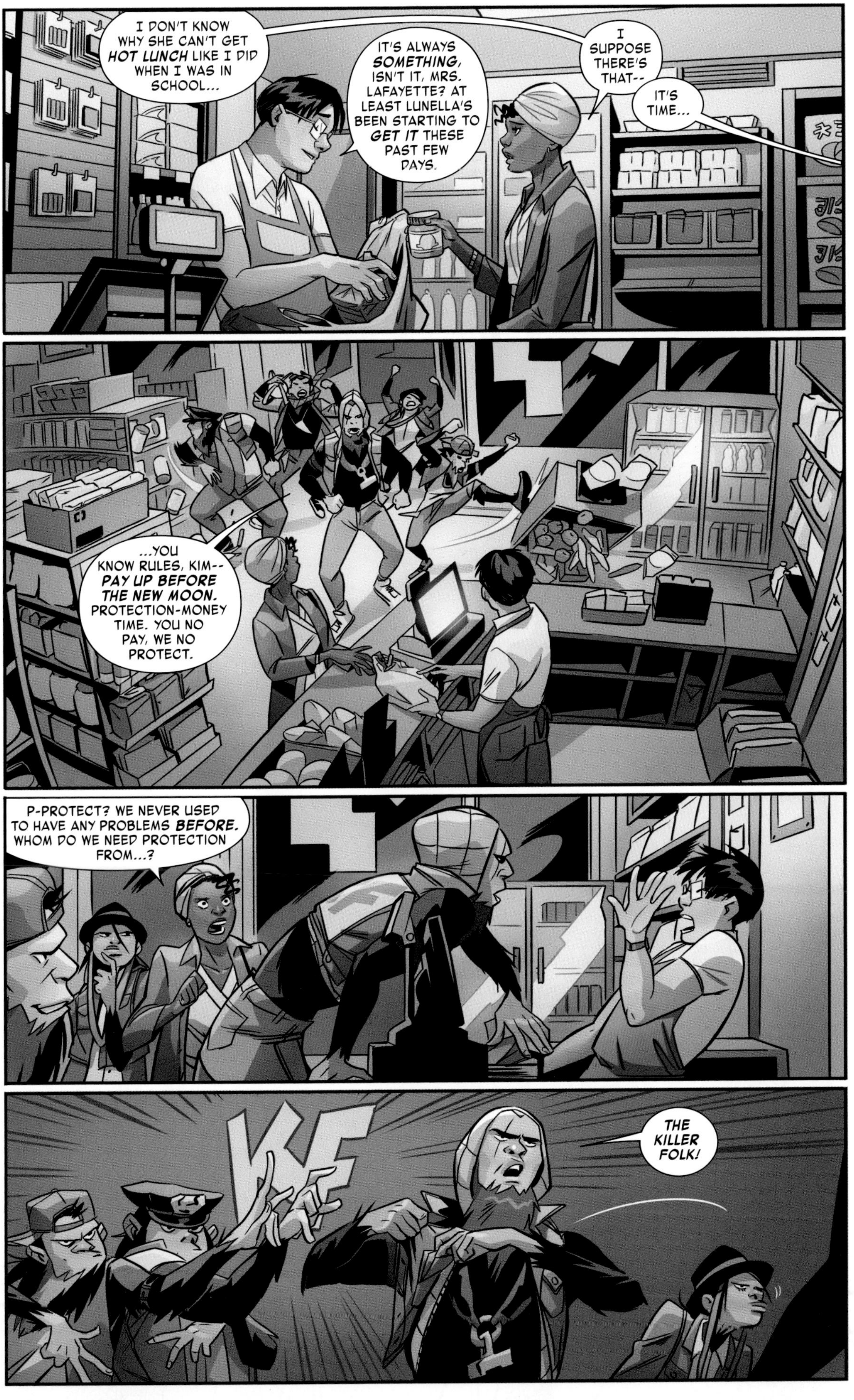
I DON'T KNOW WHY SHE CAN'T GET HOT LUNCH LIKE I DID WHEN I WAS IN SCHOOL...
IT'S ALWAYS SOMETHING, ISN'T IT, MRS. LAFAYETTE? AT LEAST LUNELLA'S BEEN STARTING TO GET IT THESE PAST FEW DAYS.
I SUPPOSE THERE'S THAT--
IT'S TIME...
...YOU KNOW RULES, KIM-- PAY UP BEFORE THE NEW MOON. PROTECTION-MONEY TIME. YOU NO PAY, WE NO PROTECT.
P-PROTECT? WE NEVER USED TO HAVE ANY PROBLEMS BEFORE. WHOM DO WE NEED PROTECTION FROM...?
THE KILLER FOLK!
KF

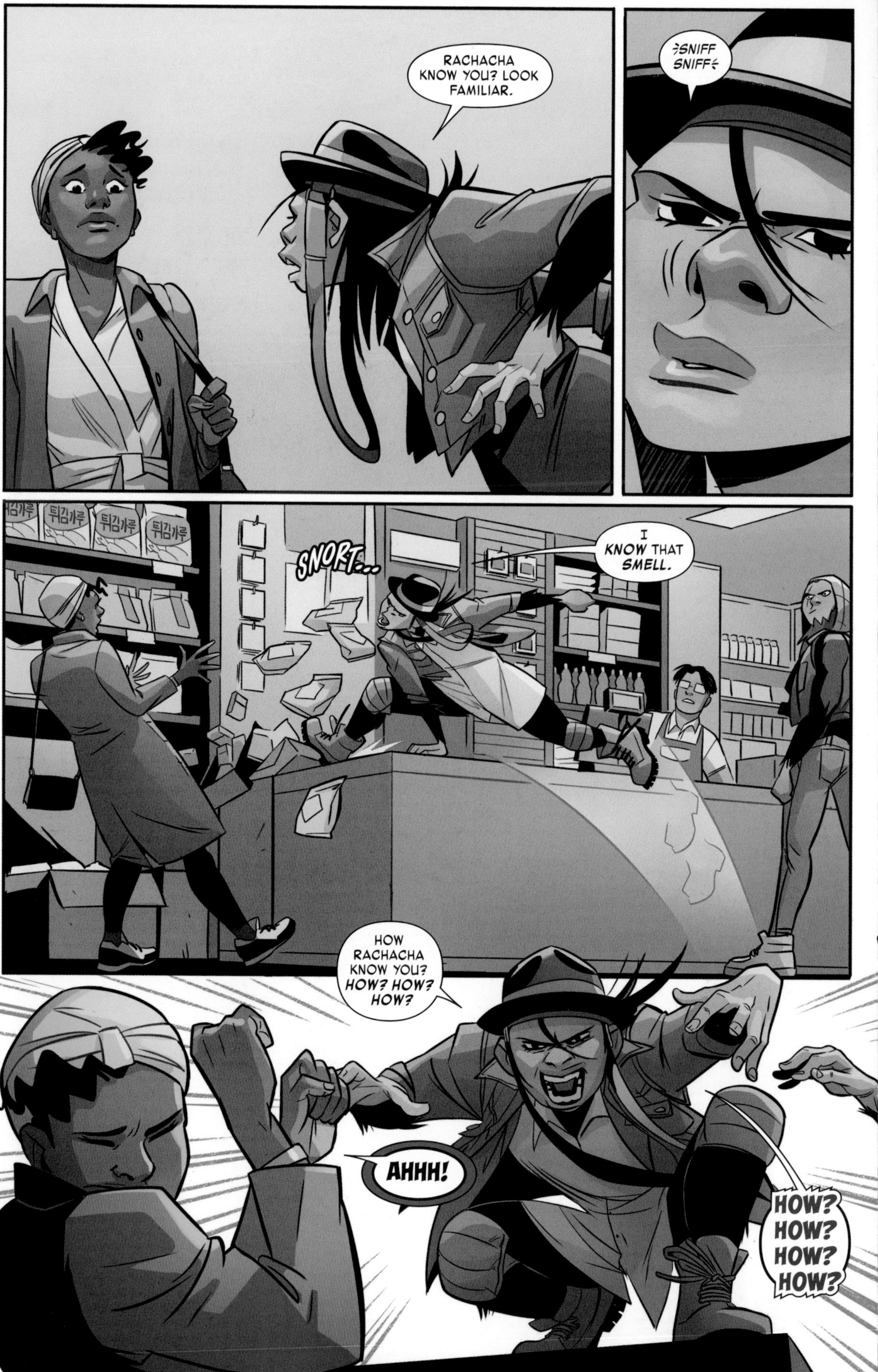
RACHACHA KNOW YOU? LOOK FAMILIAR.
⸗SNIFF SNIFF⸗
퀴김가루
튀김가루
튀김가루
튀김가루
SNORT...
I KNOW THAT SMELL.
HOW RACHACHA KNOW YOU? HOW? HOW? HOW?
AHHH!
HOW? HOW? HOW? HOW?

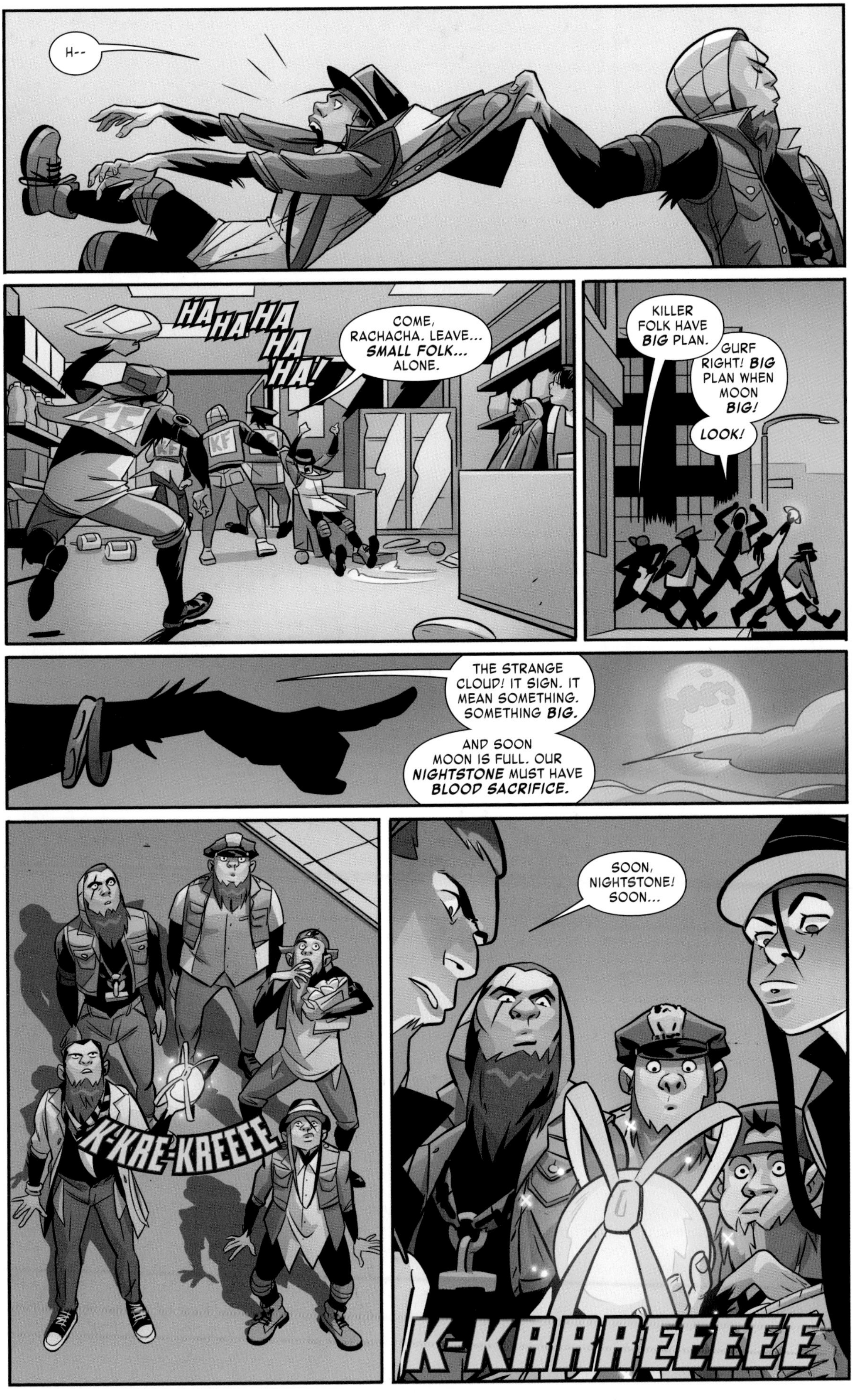
H--
HA HA HA HA HA HA!
COME, RACHACHA. LEAVE... SMALL FOLK... ALONE.
KILLER FOLK HAVE BIG PLAN.
GURF RIGHT! BIG PLAN WHEN MOON BIG!
LOOK!
THE STRANGE CLOUD! IT SIGN. IT MEAN SOMETHING. SOMETHING BIG.
AND SOON MOON IS FULL. OUR NIGHTSTONE MUST HAVE BLOOD SACRIFICE.
K-KRE-KREEEE
SOON, NIGHTSTONE! SOON...
K-KRRREEEEE

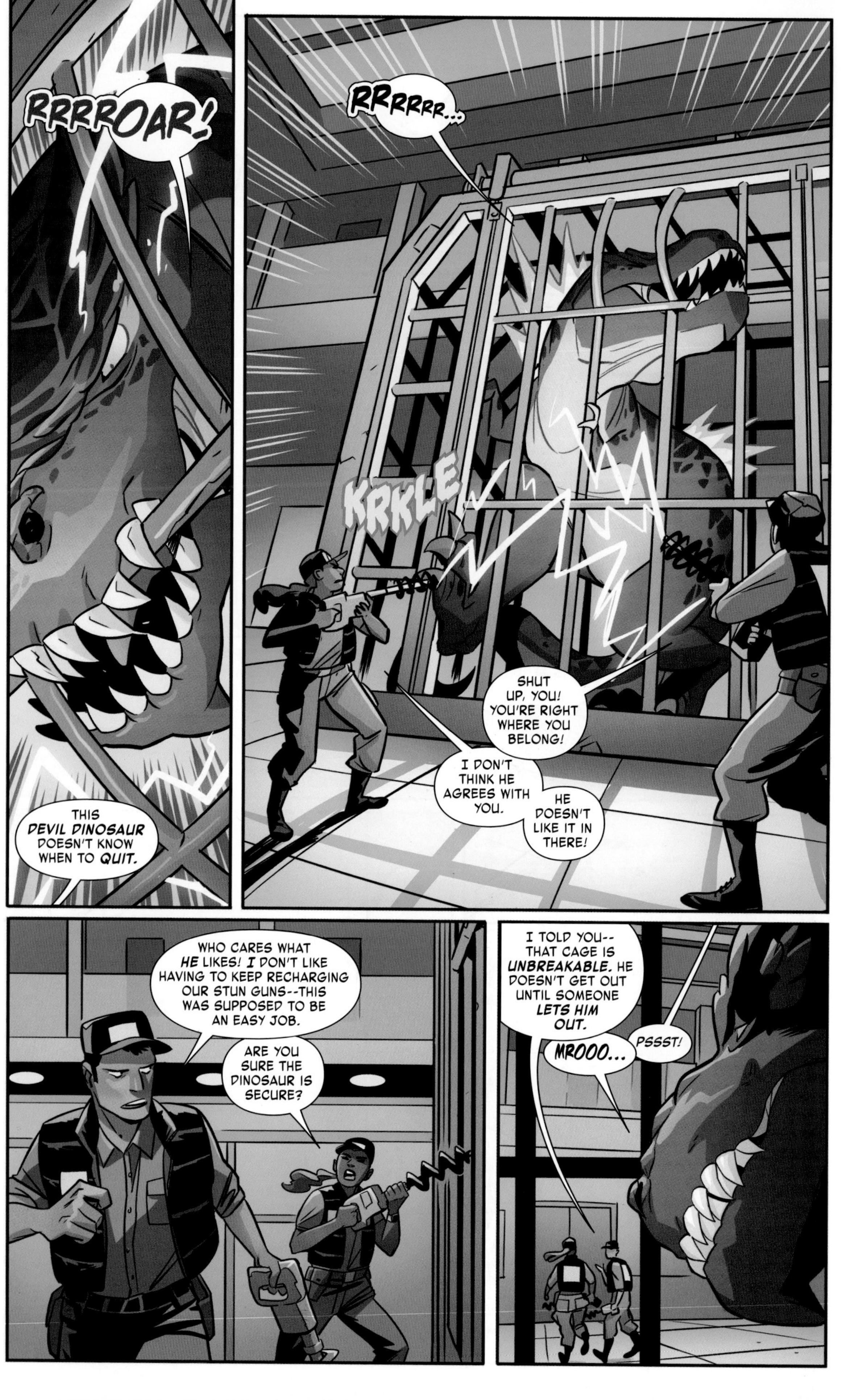
RRRROAR!
THIS DEVIL DINOSAUR DOESN'T KNOW WHEN TO QUIT.
RRRRRR...
KRKLE
SHUT UP, YOU! YOU'RE RIGHT WHERE YOU BELONG!
I DON'T THINK HE AGREES WITH YOU.
HE DOESN'T LIKE IT IN THERE!
WHO CARES WHAT HE LIKES! I DON'T LIKE HAVING TO KEEP RECHARGING OUR STUN GUNS--THIS WAS SUPPOSED TO BE AN EASY JOB.
ARE YOU SURE THE DINOSAUR IS SECURE?
I TOLD YOU--THAT CAGE IS UNBREAKABLE. HE DOESN'T GET OUT UNTIL SOMEONE LETS HIM OUT.
MROOO...
PSSST!

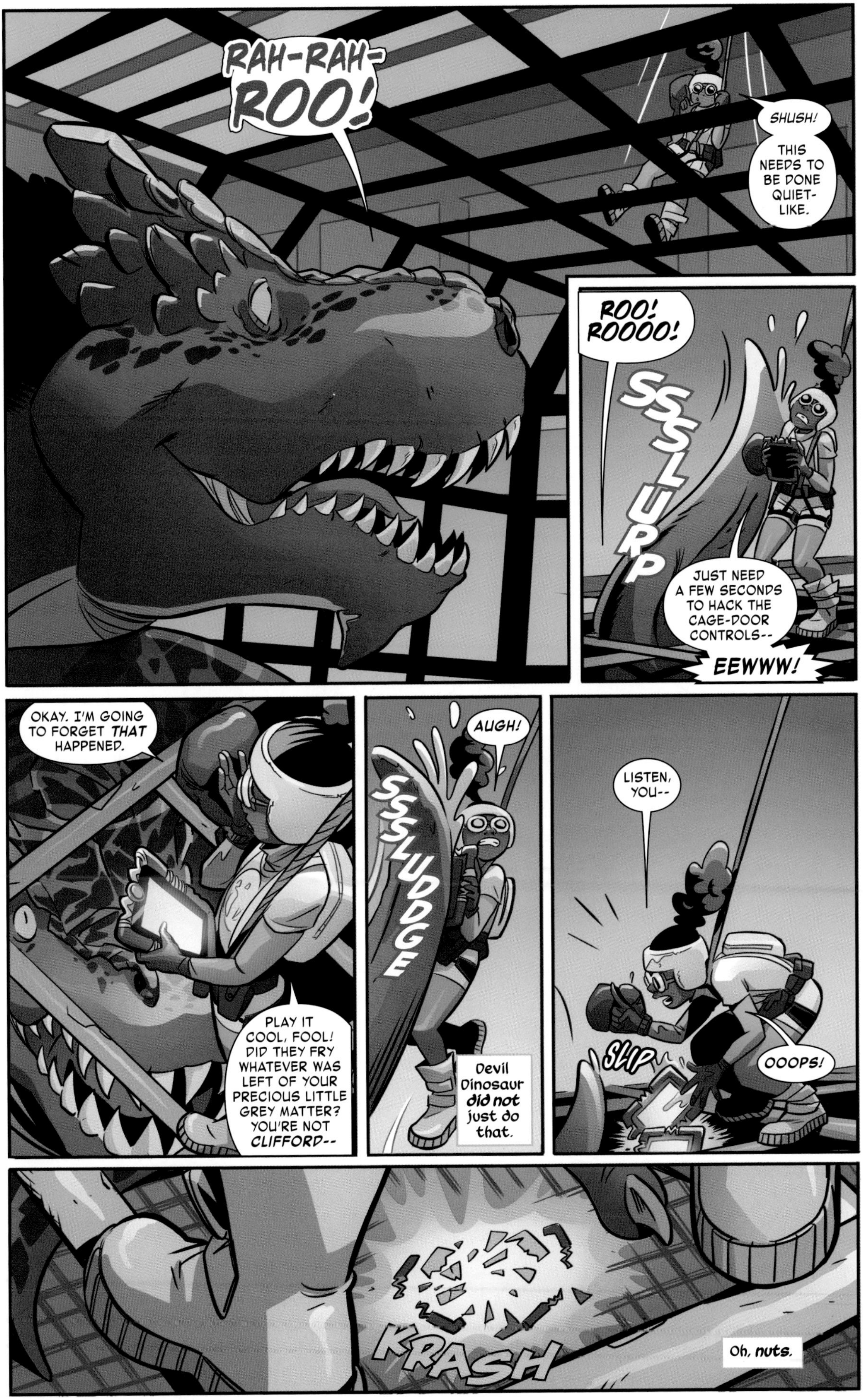
RAH-RAH-ROO!
SHUSH!
THIS NEEDS TO BE DONE QUIET-LIKE.
ROO! ROOOO!
SSSLURP
JUST NEED A FEW SECONDS TO HACK THE CAGE-DOOR CONTROLS--
EEWWW!
OKAY. I'M GOING TO FORGET THAT HAPPENED.
PLAY IT COOL, FOOL! DID THEY FRY WHATEVER WAS LEFT OF YOUR PRECIOUS LITTLE GREY MATTER? YOU'RE NOT CLIFFORD--
AUGH!
SSSLUDDGE
Devil Dinosaur did not just do that.
LISTEN, YOU--
SLIP
OOOPS!
KRASH
Oh, nuts.

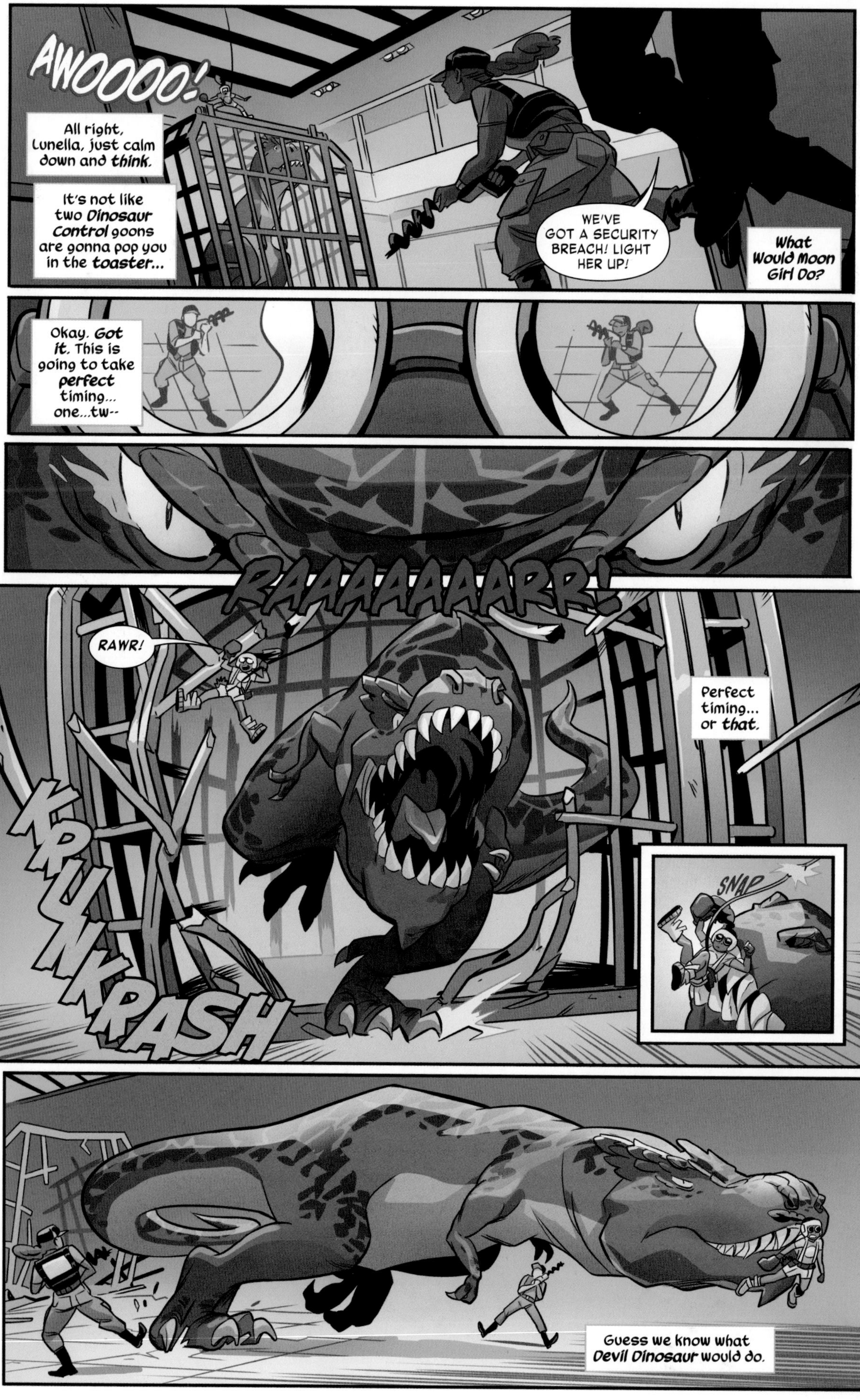
AWOOOO!
All right, Lunella, just calm down and think.
It's not like two Dinosaur Control goons are gonna pop you in the toaster...
WE'VE GOT A SECURITY BREACH! LIGHT HER UP!
What Would Moon Girl Do?
Okay. Got it. This is going to take perfect timing... one...tw--
RAAAAAAAARR!
RAWR!
Perfect timing... or that.
KRUNKRASH
SNAP
Guess we know what Devil Dinosaur would do.

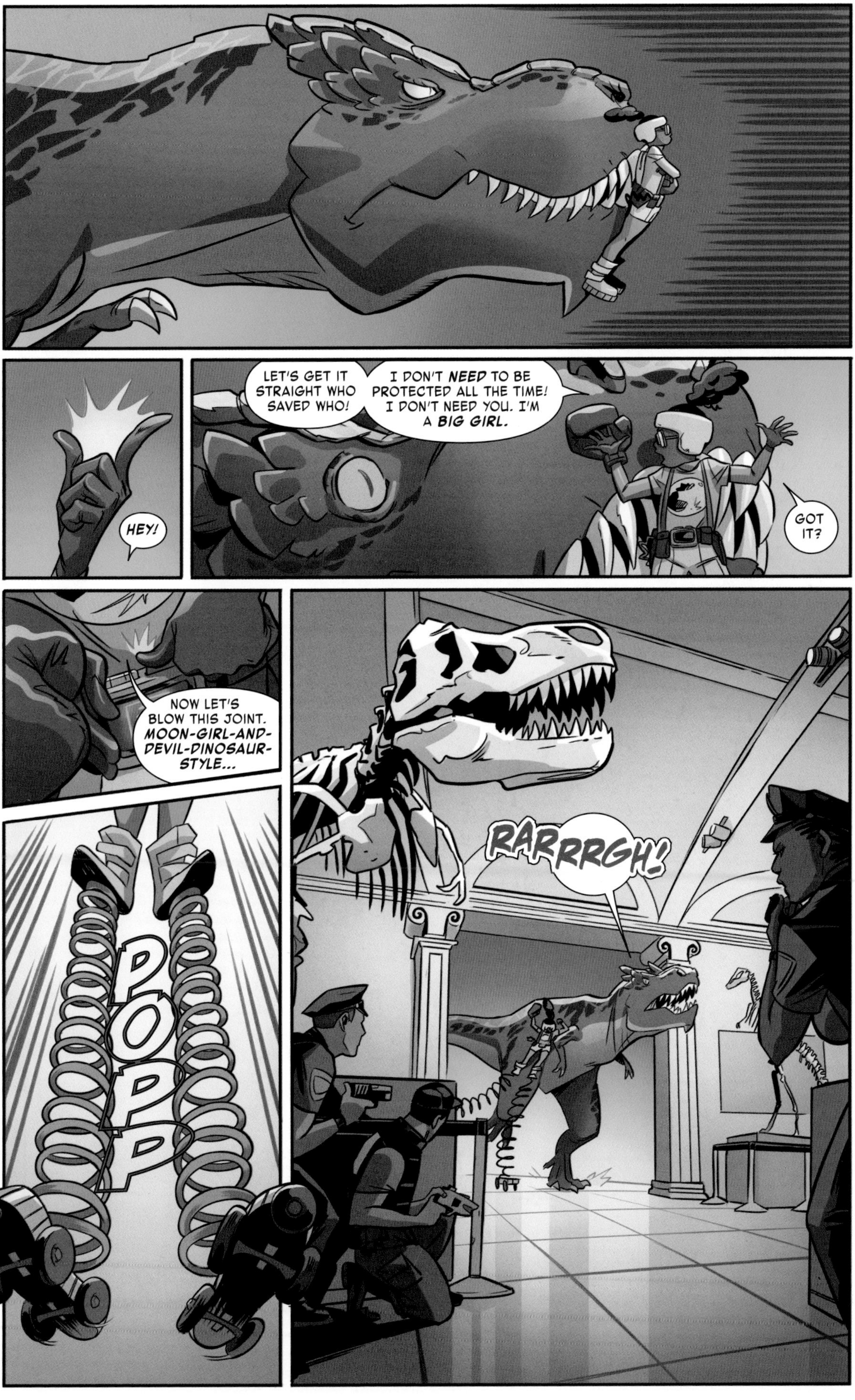
HEY!
LET'S GET IT STRAIGHT WHO SAVED WHO!
I DON'T NEED TO BE PROTECTED ALL THE TIME! I DON'T NEED YOU. I'M A BIG GIRL.
GOT IT?
NOW LET'S BLOW THIS JOINT. MOON-GIRL-AND-DEVIL-DINOSAUR-STYLE...
POPP
RARRRGH!

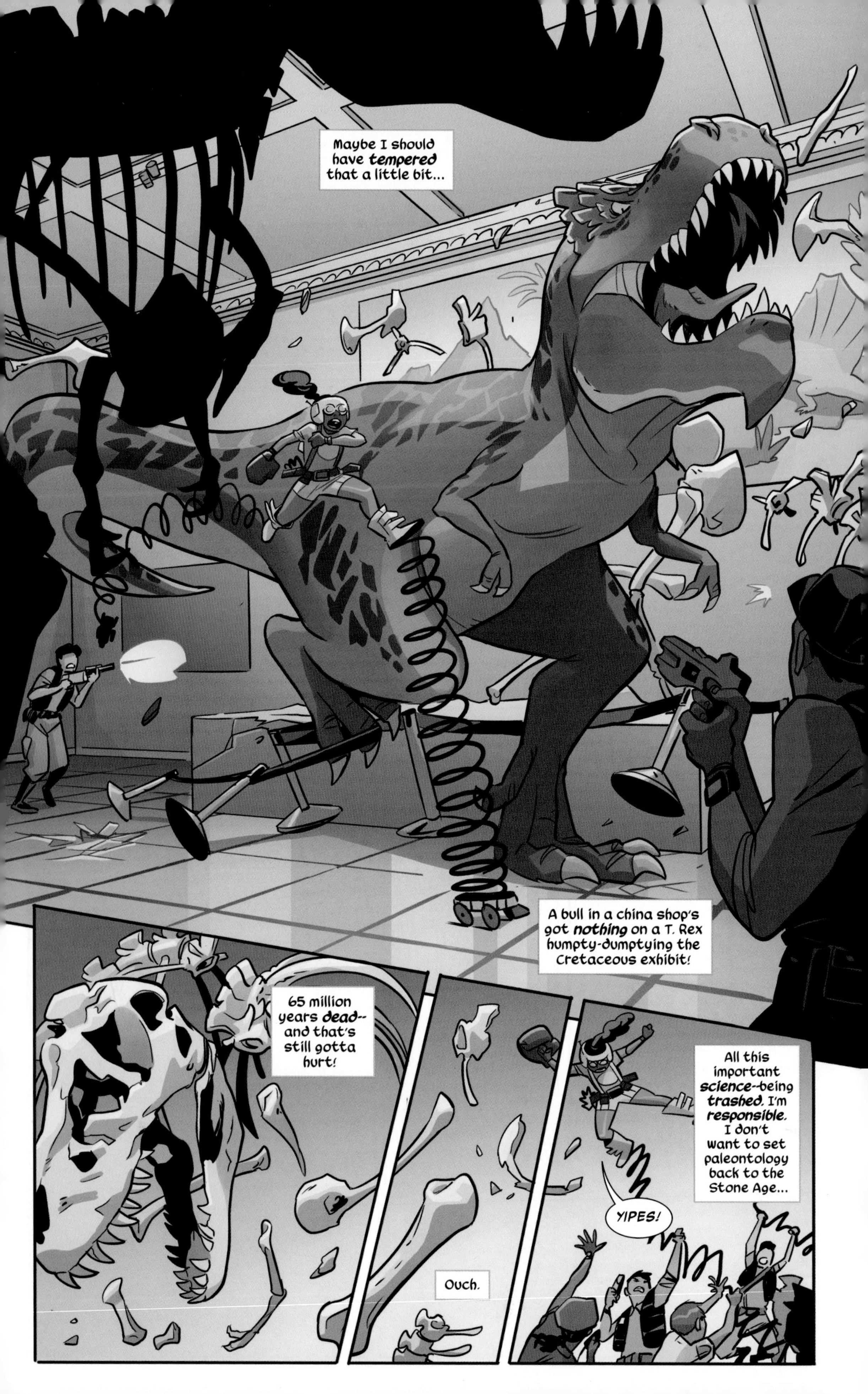
Maybe I should have *tempered* that a little bit...
A bull in a china shop's got *nothing* on a T. Rex humpty-dumptying the Cretaceous exhibit!
65 million years *dead*-- and that's still gotta hurt!
Ouch.
All this important *science*--being *trashed*. I'm *responsible*. I don't want to set paleontology back to the Stone Age...
YIPES!

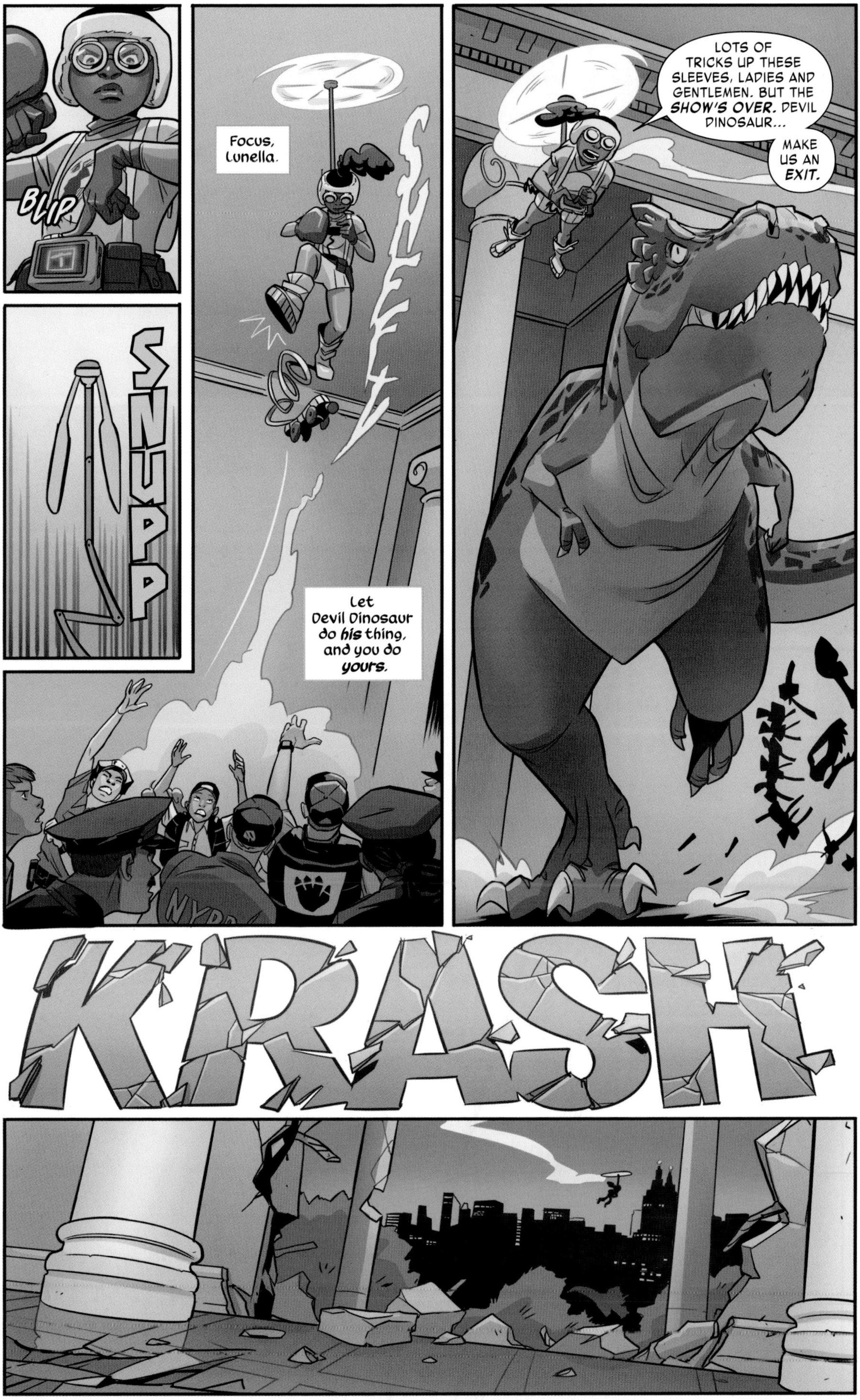

BLIP
SNUPP
Focus, Lunella.
Let Devil Dinosaur do *his* thing, and you do *yours*.
LOTS OF TRICKS UP THESE SLEEVES, LADIES AND GENTLEMEN. BUT THE ***SHOW'S OVER.*** DEVIL DINOSAUR...
MAKE US AN ***EXIT.***
KRASH

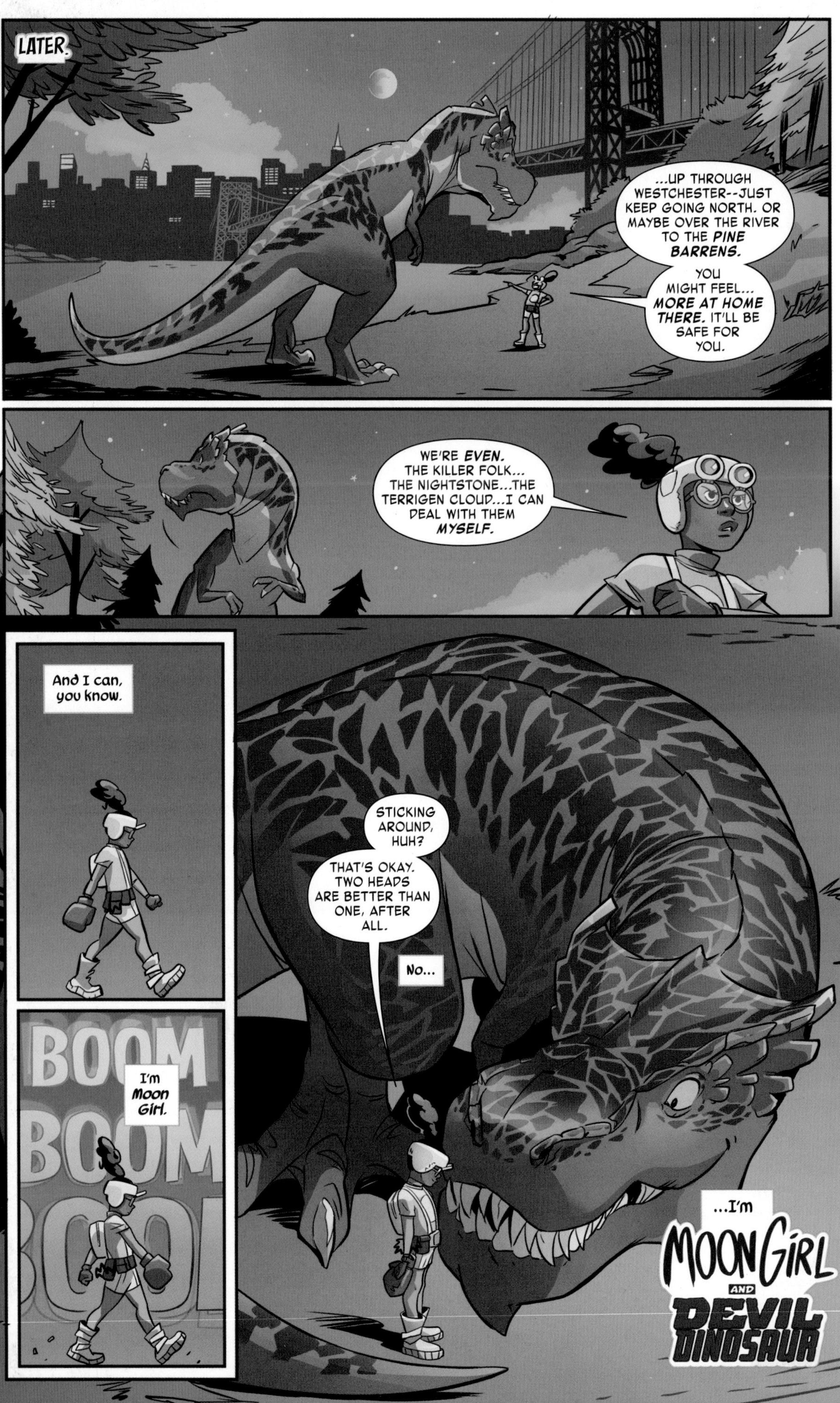
LATER.
...UP THROUGH WESTCHESTER--JUST KEEP GOING NORTH. OR MAYBE OVER THE RIVER TO THE PINE BARRENS.
YOU MIGHT FEEL... MORE AT HOME THERE. IT'LL BE SAFE FOR YOU.
WE'RE EVEN. THE KILLER FOLK... THE NIGHTSTONE...THE TERRIGEN CLOUD...I CAN DEAL WITH THEM MYSELF.
And I can, you know.
STICKING AROUND, HUH?
THAT'S OKAY. TWO HEADS ARE BETTER THAN ONE, AFTER ALL.
No...
I'm Moon Girl.
...I'm
MOON GIRL AND DEVIL DINOSAUR

MOON GIRL AND DEVIL DINOSAUR™

COLLECT THEM ALL!

Set of 6 Hardcover Books ISBN: 978-1-5321-4007-5

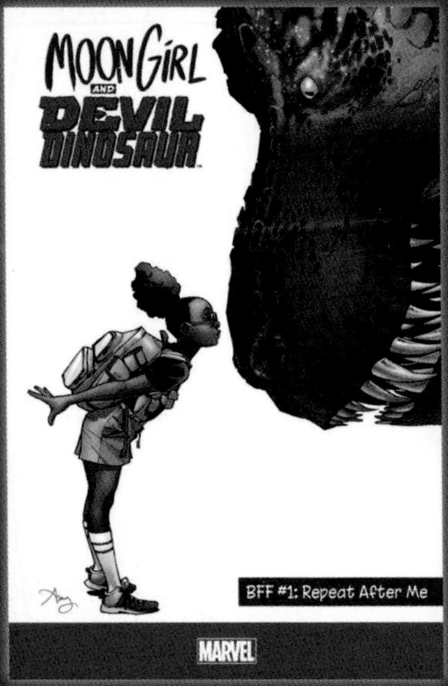
MOON GIRL AND DEVIL DINOSAUR
BFF #1: Repeat After Me
MARVEL

Hardcover Book ISBN
978-1-5321-4008-2

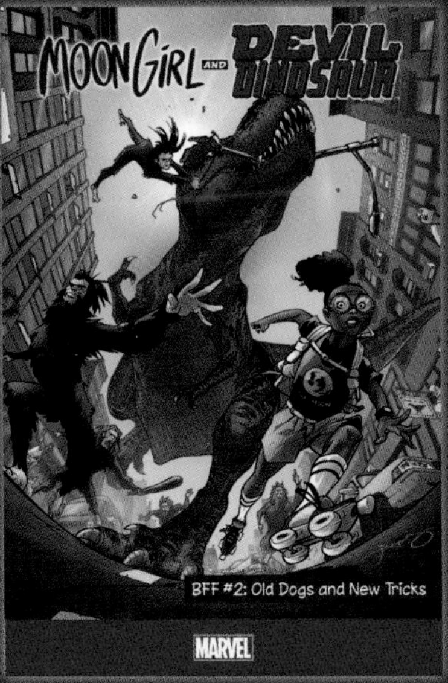
MOON GIRL AND DEVIL DINOSAUR
BFF #2: Old Dogs and New Tricks
MARVEL

Hardcover Book ISBN
978-1-5321-4009-9

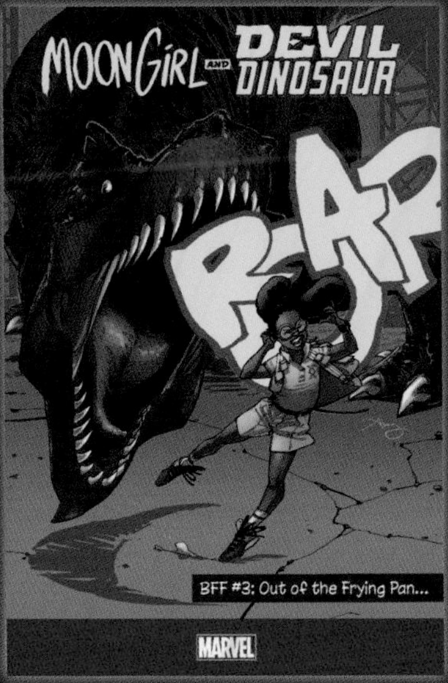
MOON GIRL AND DEVIL DINOSAUR
R-AR
BFF #3: Out of the Frying Pan...
MARVEL

Hardcover Book ISBN
978-1-5321-4010-5

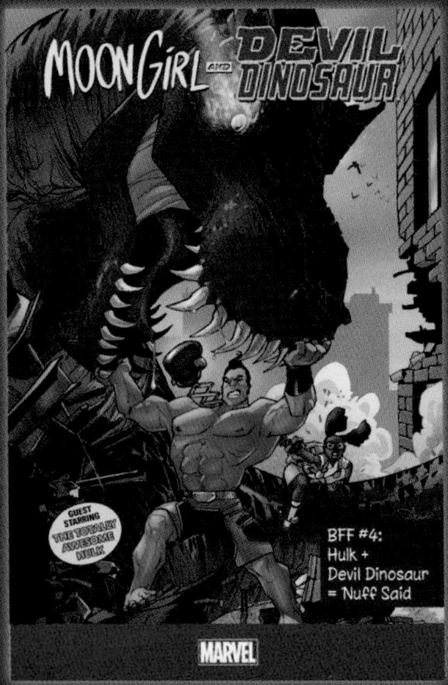
MOON GIRL AND DEVIL DINOSAUR
BFF #4: Hulk + Devil Dinosaur = Nuff Said
MARVEL

Hardcover Book ISBN
978-1-5321-4011-2

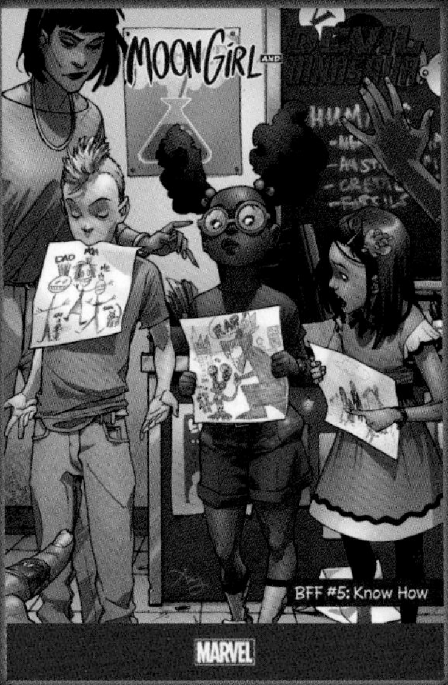
MOON GIRL AND DEVIL DINOSAUR
BFF #5: Know How
MARVEL

Hardcover Book ISBN
978-1-5321-4012-9

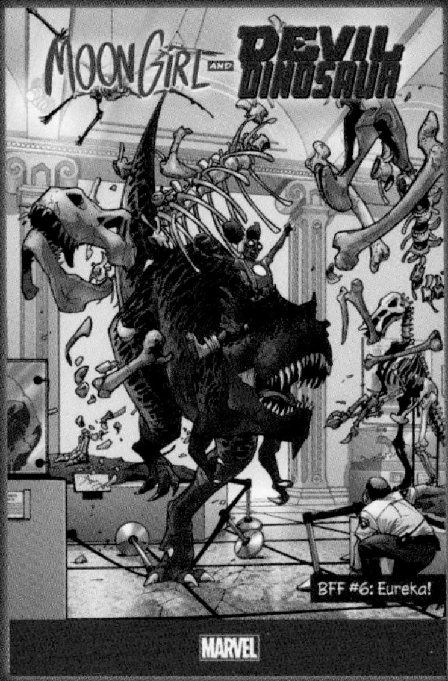
MOON GIRL AND DEVIL DINOSAUR
BFF #6: Eureka!
MARVEL

Hardcover Book ISBN
978-1-5321-4013-6